First published 2002 by Walker Books Ltd
87 Vauxhall Walk, London SE11 5HJ
2 4 6 8 10 9 7 5 3 1
© 2002 Universal Pictures Visual Programming Ltd
™ Sitting Ducks Productions
Licensed by Universal Studios Licensing LLLP
Printed in Italy
British Library Cataloguing in Publication Data:
a catalogue record for this book is available
from the British Library
ISBN 0-7445-9493-6

Denture Adventure

Story by Barbara Herndon and Jill Gorey
Adapted by Charlie Gardner

Bill had been feeling down lately — everyone was ignoring him. Ed, Oly and Waddle wouldn't listen when he told them to stop making a racket; Raoul just laughed when he asked him to turn down his music; and when Bill tried to stand up to a bullying street chicken, he was lucky to escape with his feathers.

"So that's my problem, Cecil," he confided. "Nobody listens to me. I feel like no one respects me..."

"I see," said Cecil, preoccupied with his dental X-rays.

"But y'know who they do respect?" continued Bill. "Aldo. I guess it's 'cos he's so big and green!"

"Hmm..." Cecil looked up. "Maybe it has something to do with his teeth?"

"Teeth?"

"Aldo has quite an impressive set of them, you know."

"Well that's fine for gators," Bill moaned, "but ducks don't have teeth!"

"Precisely," said Cecil. "But someday, maybe, I can change all that..."

Bill was intrigued. "What do you mean?"

Cecil looked around and lowered his voice to a whisper. "Bill, you must never reveal what I am about to show you…" Then, from a secret drawer, he produced a set of shiny plastic teeth. "Dr Cecil's Ducky Dentures! What do you think?"

"Cecil, they're magnificent!" Bill exclaimed.

"Yes they are, aren't they," said Cecil. "But they're not ready yet — they need a lot more work. You know, teeth can be dangerous things in the wrong mouth—"

"Cecil!" Claire called. "It's time to go!"

"Well, I must be off," said Cecil briskly. "Be sure to lock up when you leave…" And he rushed out, leaving Bill alone.

Bill tidied up a little, then sneaked another look in the Ducky Dentures drawer. Surely it wouldn't hurt to try them on … just once?

Bill popped in the teeth and grinned wildly into the mirror. "Bill has teeth. Teeth have power!" Cecil wouldn't mind him testing them for a bit longer, surely? Just for an hour or so...

As Bill made his way through Ducktown, he was a little too shy to smile. What if the ducks he smiled at screamed and ran away? But when a pretty female walked by, Bill couldn't resist a quick grin. For a moment, nothing happened — then her head turned and she looked at Bill again, her eyes wide open and her lashes fluttering!

Soon Bill was smiling at everyone he passed; female ducks smiled back at him while other males stepped out of the way in respect. "Wow, did you see that guy?" some ducklings squawked. "Hey, Mister, where'd ya get those teeth?" Impressed, they followed Bill along the street towards the Decoy Café.

It was a busy day in the Decoy. Bev stood in front of the counter and struggled to open a pickle jar. Suddenly the doors burst open and Bill marched in confidently, pausing for a moment to let the sunlight glint on his smile. "Hiya, Bev!" he grinned. "I'll handle that."

Bev looked up. "Bill? Is that you?" Bill snatched the jar out of her hand, bit off the lid with ease, and smiled in triumph.

"Wow! How'd he do that?" said Waddle, amazed.

"What does it matter?" replied a female customer. "I think he's adorable!"

Bev's customers were jabbering excitedly. "Hey, Bill, bite something else for us!"

"Try one of these," cooed a female admirer, tossing him a Jawbreaker. Bill caught the huge gobstopper in his teeth, winked, and shattered the sweet into pieces.
The crowd went wild. The Jawbreaker was broken!

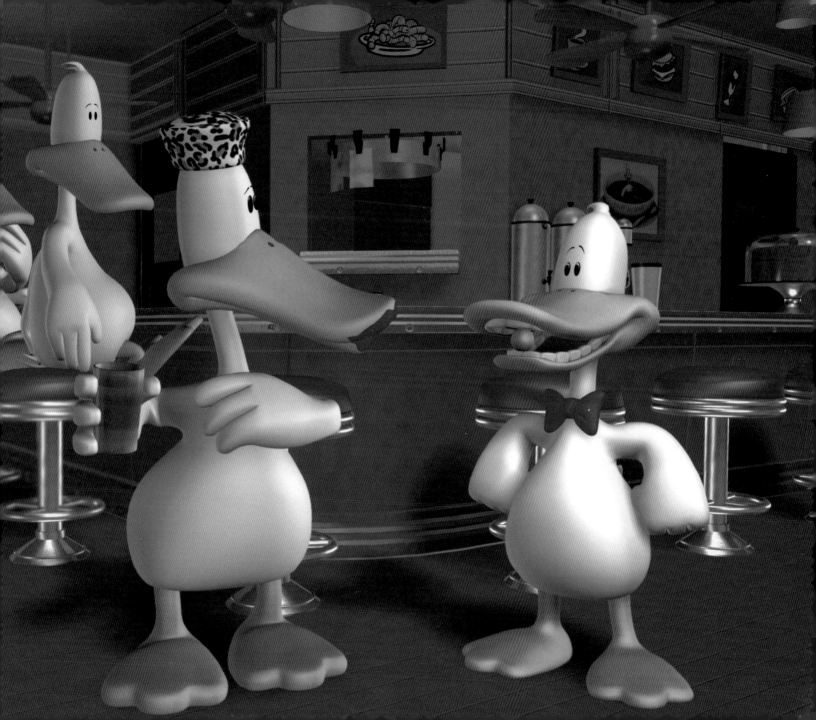

"Aldo, you should have seen me,"
Bill said that night. "For once,
everyone paid attention to me!"

Aldo eyed Bill's teeth suspiciously.
"That's great, pal. I'm happy for ya."

"These teeth make me feel like a
new duck!"

The next morning, Bill wasn't just
feeling like a new duck, he was
acting like one, too.

"Hi, cute baby!" He smiled at a
duckling in a pram. "Coochie-coo!"

"Waaaaah!" screamed the baby —
with his huge, glinting teeth Bill

looked like a dinosaur to him!

"You brute!" yelled the mother, and angrily wheeled away the pram.

Bill stopped to buy an ice cream. CRUNCH! He bit through the cornet and swallowed the ice cream in one!

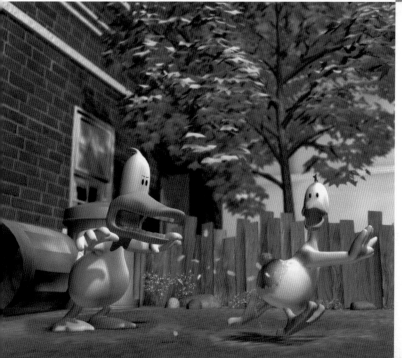

Then Bill ran into the chicken that had bullied him a few days before. "Hey! Rise and shine!" yelled Bill, his big teeth chomping menacingly. The hen jumped up and fled down the street, squawking wildly. Bill chuckled evilly and headed for the Decoy.

"Make way for the Chomper!" announced Oly, flinging open the café doors. Bill swaggered in. His teeth seemed bigger than ever — Chomper indeed!

"Bill?" asked Aldo in disbelief.

Too scared to eat, several ducks got up and left; Ed, Oly and Waddle gobbled down their leftovers.

Raoul was dancing to a song on the juke-box. Bill didn't like the tune, so — CHOMP! — he took a bite right out of the music centre.

"Hey there, pal," said Aldo bravely. "Why not get rid of those teeth?"

Bill gave him a hard stare. "And why would I want do that?"

"Because you're scarin' ducklings and chomping the furniture," said Aldo, annoyed by Bill's attitude. "Nobody likes you any more!"

"Can I help it if everyone's jealous? At least they respect me now."

"Bill, buddy, they don't respect you … they're afraid of you." Aldo got up to pay. "Look, I gotta go. Just think about what I said, OK?"

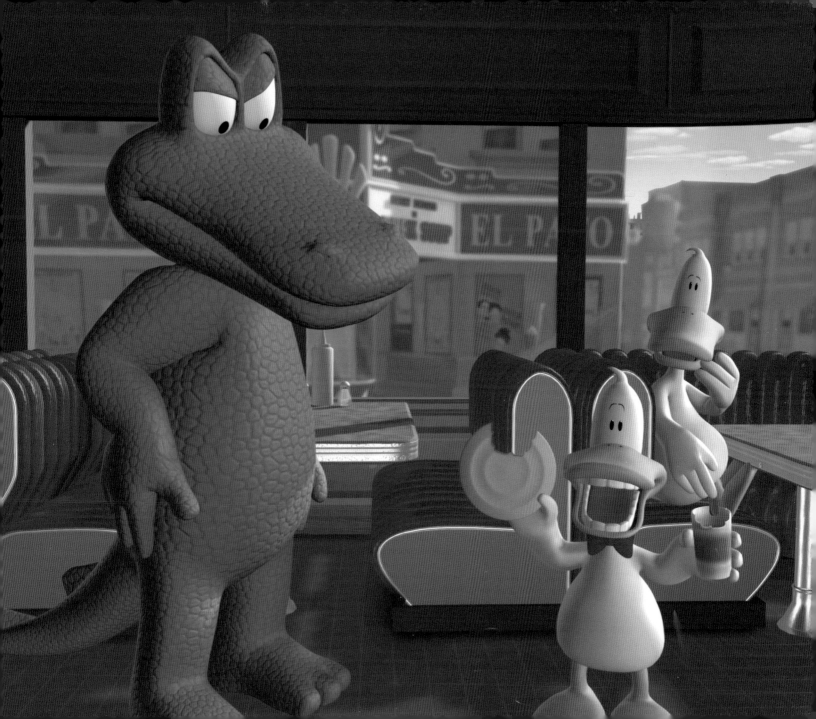

A little later, Bill left the café determined to prove Aldo wrong. He grinned at the ducklings that had liked his teeth so much. Terrified, they ran away round the corner.

Then Bill saw the chicken again. "Howdy!" he began, hoping to apologize. "Say, about our last little..." But the chicken just screamed and hid in a litter bin.

Bill was starting to feel alone and unwanted. He caught sight of his reflection in a shop window. Were those really his teeth? Even he was a little frightened.

Suddenly he remembered Aldo's advice in the café: "They don't respect you, they're afraid of you ... afraid of you..."

"Oh my gosh!" Bill exclaimed. "What have I become? Aldo's right!" He popped the teeth out of his mouth, and for the first time that day he felt like his old self again. "The sooner I get these back to Cecil's, the better!"

"Wha's your hurry, Signor Chomper?" Raoul swooped out of nowhere and snatched the dentures from Bill's grasp. "First, I like to test-drive the big teeth!"

"Hey, give those back!" Bill chased after him and grabbed onto the crow's leg.

Raoul flapped harder and lifted Bill off the ground. "Leggo, duck!"

"Not until you give me those teeth! You don't know how dangerous they are!"

But Raoul wouldn't listen. He dragged Bill behind him, shunting him first into a post-box, then a fire hydrant, then a traffic sign. But still Bill held on. Eventually, the two birds got into a tussle atop a statue.

"Give — them — back!" Bill demanded, grabbing them from Raoul.

"Make — me!" Raoul yanked them back, then lost his grip. Bill lunged to catch them, and fell off the branch. SPLOOCH! Bill thudded to the ground. BOING! The teeth bounced off a branch and into his mouth.

Bill came round — and blinked. He could hardly believe his eyes. Raoul was standing over him ... and his mouth was full of teeth! "Bye-bye, Biiiiiiiiill!" he laughed, and flew off.

"Hey! Come back!" yelled Bill, giving chase. He spotted a police-duck on a scooter. "Officer, that bird stole my... Aaaagh!" The officer had a mouth full of teeth too!

Bill ran for his life. What had he done? Everyone he passed had teeth. Young, old, male and female — even the chickens had teeth. Worse still, they were using them! Crowds of ducks were biting through anything in sight: streetlamps, fences, dustbins and scooters... Ducktown was being chomped to pieces!

* * *

"Wake up, little buddy!" said Aldo's voice, inside Bill's head. "Bill, wake up..."

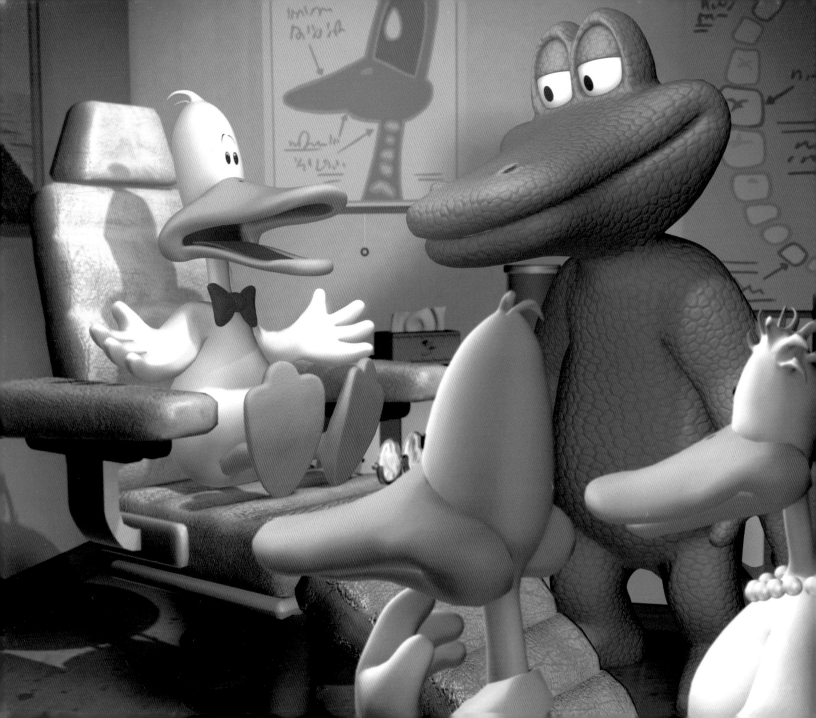

Bill awoke to find himself in a Dr Cecil's surgery. Aldo and Claire were standing by him. "Wh-what happened?" he murmured.

"We found you in the park," Aldo explained. "You had the teeth jammed in your mouth, but Cecil got them out." Cecil waved the dentures reassuringly.

"Aldo, Cecil, it was horrible!" Bill shuddered. "Everyone in Ducktown had huge teeth! They were chomping everything in sight!"

"Don't worry, Bill," comforted Cecil, "it was only a dream..."

"But I had teeth, didn't I? I turned into a bully and nobody liked me..."

Aldo grinned. "That part was true."

"Then I guess I owe everyone an apology. Especially you, Cecil."

"No worries," Cecil replied. "I think the Ducky Dentures need a bit more development. Anyway, we all forgive you..."

"But hey, little buddy," Aldo smiled, "don't bite off more than you can chew!"

And the toothy alligator and the three toothless ducks laughed and laughed and laughed.